For sure it brightens your day ...
Laugh out Loud...

CONTENT

Chapter 1 : *The Selfie Gone Wrong*   5

Chapter 2 : *The Social Media Mix-Up*   8

Chapter 3 : *The Time-Travelling Mishap*   11

Chapter 4 : *The TikTok Challenge Fiasco*   15

Chapter 5 : *The Virtual Reality Vortex*   19

Chapter 6 : *The Wacky Pet Competition* 23

Chapter 7 : *The Robot Roommate*   27

Chapter 8   : The Misadventures of a
              Delivery Driver   31

Chapter 9   : The Unbelievable
              Substitute Teacher   35

Chapter 10 : The Magical Mischief
              Maker   40

Chapter 11 : The Case of the Missing
              Socks   44

Chapter 12 : The Prankster's Revenge   48

Chapter 13 : The Disastrous Cooking
              Class   52

Chapter 14 : The Unforgettable School
              Trip   56

Chapter 15 : The Case of the Mysterious
              Locker   60

Chapter 16 : The Haunted House
              Sleepover   64

Chapter 17 : *The Great Candy Caper*   68

Chapter 18 : *The Doggy Disaster*   72

Chapter 19 : *The Hilarious Talent Show Act*   76

Chapter 20 : *The Case of the Talking Toilet*   80

"The Selfie Gone Wrong"

Emma was a teenager who formerly resided in the bustling town of Millbrook. She was a typical high school girl who enjoyed taking selfies to record her life. Emma was known for always getting the ideal photo, and her Instagram followers were jealous of her.

She made the decision to go to the neighbourhood park on a bright Saturday afternoon. She decided it would be the ideal time to take a selfie while surrounded by the beauty of nature because the weather was right. She had no idea that her good intentions would result in a humorous and uncomfortable situation.

Emma came to the park prepared to strike a number of postures with her dependable smartphone in hand. She located a charming location close to a tranquil pond where ducks were lazily swimming. She put the camera to her face and got ready for her famously seductive smile, her excitement brimming.

A strong blast of wind passed by just as Emma was ready to press the shutter, throwing her off balance. She lost her balance and unintentionally dropped her phone. She stretched out in a rush to grab it, but inadvertently hit herself in the face.

Unbeknownst to Emma, her phone had taken a rapid-fire series of pictures of the entire occurrence. She swiftly reached down to pick up her phone while blushing with shame. She had no idea that her blunder had produced a collection of amusing and true photos.

She gave in to her curiosity, and Emma made the decision to look through the pictures. She scanned the pictures in anticipation of finding her perfect selfie. Instead, she started laughing uncontrollably. Her wide-eyed expression of surprise could be seen in the photographs, along with her hand flailing in the air and her amusingly distorted face.

Emma couldn't help but laugh and posted the pictures on Instagram with the message, "When your selfie game takes an unexpected turn! #EpicFail." Her pals found the post to be hysterically funny and started commenting and loving it almost immediately.

She was shocked when her botched selfie became viral in a matter of hours. Numerous people shared and reposted the images, which led to their eventual virality. Her real and understandable moment of awkwardness entertained people from all around the world.

Emma accepted her new identity as the woman with the epic selfie fail as the fame grew. She began posting more amusing and lighter stuff and gained a reputation for being able to laugh at herself. Her social media following grew rapidly, and she even caught the interest of companies looking to work with her.

She gained valuable knowledge about accepting flaws and finding humour in unexpected circumstances through this unexpected turn of events. She became an example for others, encouraging them to laugh at their own mistakes and not take themselves too seriously.

Emma's disastrous selfie thus not only made others laugh, but it also gave her a greater understanding of the value of an authentic, unfiltered moment and the beauty of imperfection. She made everyone smile, one selfie at a time, starting the next day by sharing her special perspective with the globe.

"The Social Media Mix-Up"

There was a teenager named Max who lived in the world of hashtags, likes, and retweets. Max loved social media and was constantly following the newest trends and trying to amuse his followers. He was, however, the victim of a humorous social media mix-up one fateful day.

Everything began innocently enough when Max chose to mail his best friend Sarah with a humorous and slightly awkward message. On the well-known social media site Chirper, he had intended to send her a private direct message. Max started frantically typing, creating a clever message about a humorous thing that had happened at school earlier that day.

Lily, Max's younger sister, had borrowed his phone earlier and altered several of his Chirper settings without his knowledge. As a practical joke, she had changed Sarah's name to that of their eccentric neighbour Mr. Jenkins in Max's contacts' display names.

Lily handed Max the phone back with a sly smirk, not realising the confusion he would encounter. Max chose the contact he thought was Sarah and sent the message without giving the switcheroo much attention.

8

Max was completely perplexed by the reaction he got a short while later. "Hello, young man," it said. Do you mean the situation with the squirrel? Very strange, in fact. Max pondered the letter, wondering how Sarah knew about squirrels as he peered at it in confusion. At that point, he understood that his communication had actually gone to Mr. Jenkins rather than Sarah at all.

Max swiftly read through his texts while in a panic and saw the error. Realising that the incorrect person had heard his embarrassing story, he groaned in frustration. Instead of being embarrassed, he found himself laughing out loud at how ridiculous the situation was.

Max messaged Mr. Jenkins, clarifying the mix-up and apologising for the confusion, deciding to embrace the humorous mishap. To his astonishment, Mr. Jenkins replied with a smile and related a funny story of his own. It turns out that Mr. Jenkins enjoyed observing squirrels and had plenty of entertaining tales to tell.

Max was in awe of his good fortune. What had first been a humiliating error had now developed into an oddball internet connection with his neighbour. They kept exchanging messages, and each one was funnier than the last. As soon as the Chirper community heard about their humorous talks, the hashtag #SquirrelsAndLaughs started to gain popularity.

Max and Mr. Jenkins planned a neighbourhood meeting in response to their growing notoriety, inviting everyone to share their funniest animal encounters. Laughter, funny anecdotes, and a rekindled sense of camaraderie pervaded the occasion.

Max, on the other hand, realised that the social media blunder had taught him a valuable lesson about finding humour in unexpected circumstances and establishing relationships with others via shared laughter. He persisted in conversing with his audience, offering funny anecdotes and urging them to enjoy life's oddities and mistakes.

Max and Mr. Jenkins so demonstrated that even a tiny error could result in fantastic friendships and non stop laughing from a simple social media mix-up. Their encounter became a shining example of how a little humour may make an awkward mistake into a fun and memorable event.

"The Time-Travelling Mishap"

A young man named Ethan used to reside in the sleepy town of Willowville. He had always imagined doing something amazing because he possessed a mind that was bursting with curiosity and a talent for experimenting. His aspirations came true one fateful day when he finished building a time machine in his disorganised garage.

Ethan was so excited he couldn't help but want to test his idea straight immediately. He climbed inside the svelte, metallic machine and entered an arbitrary date on the console. He saw himself speeding through time as a series of lights and sounds flashed.

He stepped out of the machine as the dust settled and it came to a stop, hoping to enter a brand-new and fascinating period. He was shocked to discover himself in the middle of a busy circus. A ringmaster shouted through a loudhailer as clowns and acrobats performed in the air.

Ethan chose to embrace the unexpected era and immerse himself in the circus atmosphere despite his confusion. He joined the group, donning a vibrant costume and joining the acrobats in risky routines. Ethan's excitement and inherent sense of humour won the crowd over despite his lack of expertise.

He had to use his comedic timing on one particular occasion. He suddenly found himself juggling bowling pins, riding a unicycle, and dodging a cheeky monkey that had escaped from its cage. Ethan couldn't help but join in the commotion as the audience burst out laughing.

The monkey jumped onto his head just as he felt he had perfected the juggling act, throwing him off-balance. He fell off the unicycle and hit a pile of foam stage props. The audience burst into even louder laughter after misunderstanding the incident for a joke.

Ethan picked himself up and joined in the laughs after realising that sometimes the best moments were the ones that didn't go as planned. He accepted his part as the awkward yet endearing entertainer, and the circus quickly turned into his second home.

Weeks passed by as Ethan grew accustomed to the exciting circus lifestyle. With the circus troupe, each member of which had their own peculiarities and skills, he grew close. Together, they enthralled audiences night after night with a tornado of delight and laughter.

Even though Ethan loved living the circus life, he couldn't deny the want to go back home. He said goodbye to his new pals with a heavy heart and got back into the time machine, ready to travel back in time once more.

Ethan got ready for the next location as the time machine started up. However, as luck would have it, a malfunction happened and sent him whirling across several centuries. After experiencing disco fever in the 1970s, he then found himself in ancient Egypt, and finally in a futuristic society with flying cars.

Ethan met several comical events during his time-travelling travels. With flapper girls, he danced the Charleston; with perplexed Egyptians, he attempted to read hieroglyphics; and in platform shoes, he grooved to disco tunes.

The time machine finally came to a stop after a series of humorous blunders, and Ethan was thrust back into his own time. He was in awe of the dizzying array of experiences he had gone through as he exited the machine.

Although Ethan set out to create a time machine, he had no idea that the errors and unexpected eras would provide for the funniest stories and most memorable experiences. He had discovered that the best adventures in life frequently occur when things don't go according to plan, whether they be in the circus, ancient Egypt, or the disco era.

With a gleam in his eye, Ethan made a promise to treasure the spontaneous moments and welcome the unexpected in his daily life. After all, the real adventures were found in those times of chaos and hilarity.

"The TikTok Challenge Fiasco"

Once upon a time, a bunch of friends got together at Lily's house for a fun-filled afternoon in the small town of Oakville. Since they were all devoted TikTok users, Lily, Jake, Mia, and Max were unable to resist the most recent viral challenge that had taken the internet by storm—the "Dance Craze Mashup."

The pals gathered in Lily's living room with their cellphones in hand, ready to demonstrate their best dance moves in an attempt to make their own funny take on the challenge. They were determined to master the sophisticated choreography, so they watched the film frame by frame and carefully analysed each move.

The pals began their act by pressing the record button while exuding confidence. But as luck would have it, things swiftly went astray. During their coordinated movements, Jake's foot got snagged on the rug's edge and he fell into Mia.

Their dancing performance devolved into an absurd clash of writhing bodies and flailing limbs. A spontaneous slapstick comedy routine between the friends caused the entire room to break out in laughter. Unintentionally, their botched attempt at the TikTok challenge turned into the funniest video they had ever made.

The buddies chose to embrace the humour and post their blooper film on TikTok with the tagline, "When your dance challenge goes hilariously wrong! #EpicFail," unfazed by their misfortune. They had no idea that their film would quickly become popular online and make people chuckle.

The gang found itself in the limelight of TikTok stardom as the video grew in popularity. They received comments and requests for more interesting stuff from people all around the world. The guys recognised a chance to showcase their distinct brand of humour by coming up with a series of hilarious tasks that went wrong.

Lily, Jake, Mia, and Max set out on a mission to make the funniest and most ridiculous TikTok challenge videos in response to their sudden notoriety. A chair toppling, a wardrobe malfunction, or a surprise photobomb by Lily's cheeky pet cat marred each attempt.

The friends gained more fans and laughter with each mishap. As they discussed how to surpass their previous difficulties, their living room turned into a centre of insanity and innovation. Their videos were bursting with infectious laughter, shocking turns, and the pure joy of friendship.

However, despite the laughter and fame, the buddies never lost sight of the primary purpose of their videos—to provide their viewers joy and a fun vacation. People sent them notes from all around the world, explaining how their movies had made their days happier and served as a reminder to rejoice in life's unexpected moments.

As the challenges went on, their notoriety grew outside of TikTok. They were given the opportunity to showcase their experience of transforming bad dance steps into comic gold on chat shows. As the "quadruple of laughter," Lily, Jake, Mia, and Max encouraged others to embrace their flaws and find humour in their own lives.

In the end, what mattered most was the actual connections they formed with people via laughter, not just their notoriety or the number of likes they earned. With each humorous error, their friendship became closer, and they came to understand that the actual TikTok challenge wasn't about getting it perfect, but about having fun and sharing happiness.

The TikTok Challenge Fiasco evolved into a fable about friendship, humour, and the ability to find joy despite disaster. One amusing incident at a time, Lily, Jake, Mia, and Max continued their journey while making films that made people grin all over the world.

"The Virtual Reality Vortex"

A young man named Alex used to reside in the sleepy hamlet of Techville. Alex loved playing video games and was constantly looking for the next big adventure. Alex was eager to explore the immersive world when the brand-new virtual reality game "Vortex Quest" debuted.

Alex slipped on the stylish VR gear and stepped into the Vortex Quest virtual world. The game promised breathtaking scenery, grand adventures, and never-ending excitement. Alex had no idea that this journey would be much more than he had imagined.

As Alex progressed further in the game, the virtual setting started to change and take on surprising shapes. Alex discovered themselves in a weird, cartoonish environment rather than the stunning scenery that had been promised. The ground was composed of shaky gelatin, the trees were rainbow-coloured, and the sky was covered in flying pizza pieces.

He made the decision to investigate this odd virtual reality vortex despite his confusion. They were propelled into the air and into a treehouse inhabited by talking monkeys wearing tuxedos as Alex took a step forward, causing the earth beneath their feet to quake like a trampoline.

Alex started a spirited dialogue with the monkeys, who insisted on instructing them in the art of banana juggling, and was startled yet pleased by their antics. They couldn't help but giggle at the ridiculousness of the scenario, even though juggling bananas wasn't exactly the noble goal Alex had in mind.

After saying goodbye to the monkeys, Alex continued his search for a method to return to reality. The virtual world threw new curveballs at me with each step. Alex found themselves in a pleasant wrestling bout with a sentient mound of goo, a tea party with three singing rabbits, and a dance-off with pixelated aliens.

Despite these absurd meetings, Alex's will to get home never faltered. Alex accepted the laughter and revelled in the unexpected as the virtual reality tornado continued tossing anomalies their way.

After a succession of amusing and perplexing obstacles, Alex eventually came across a doorway that appeared to shine with a familiar glow. They jumped into the portal without thinking, expecting it would take them back to the real world.

Alex returned to their own room with the VR headgear still securely fastened as the dazzling light faded. They became confused, wondering if it had all been a dream. However, they soon became aware of a small problem with the space: banana peel wallpaper covering the walls, a neon sign flashing "Rabbit Rendezvous," and a puddle of vibrant goo on the floor.

He started to realise. There were still signs of the whimsical turmoil of the virtual reality vortex, which had briefly blended with the physical world. Alex laughed hysterically instead of becoming anxious, enjoying the odd memento of their voyage.

From that moment on, Alex's outlook on life was one of humour and adventure. They had learned to accept the unexpected and have fun even in the most absurd circumstances thanks to the virtual reality vortex.

And so, with a sly glitter in their eyes, Alex carried on with their gaming exploits, exploring fresh virtual worlds. The Virtual Reality Vortex became a fable among gamers, serving as a reminder that spontaneity and humour may be discovered not just in the virtual world but also in the erratic turns of daily life.

"The Wacky Pet Competition"

There once was a teen named Emily who resided in the town of Whimsyville. Emily had a pet to match her eccentric attitude, which she had always been renowned for. She had a strange little friend named Fuzzbert who was a lovable cross between a dog, a cat, and a hamster.

Emily came upon a flier for the annual Wacky Pet Competition one day. She was excited when she realised that this was the ideal chance to highlight Fuzzbert's special abilities. Emily entered the contest with a determined sparkle in her eye.

As the competition day approached, Emily and Fuzzbert made their way to the park hosting the gathering. As people from all walks of life gathered there with their eccentric dogs, the atmosphere was teeming with anticipation. There were superhero-themed canines, parrots riding tiny bicycles, and even a goldfish with piano-playing abilities.

As she turned to face Fuzzbert, Emily muttered, "Okay, buddy, it's time to show everyone what you've got." Fuzzbert gave an enthusiastic squeak in return, eager to bask in the limelight.

The competition kicked off with a parade of eccentric animals performing. Cats crossed a tightrope, dogs leapt through hoops, while birds did acrobatics. The audience applauded and clapped as they were astounded by the amazing ability on exhibit.

When it was Fuzzbert's turn, Emily frightenedly escorted him to the stage's centre. As Emily signalled for Fuzzbert to execute his first trick—a somersault—the spotlight shone down on them. The crowd laughed as Fuzzbert spun in the air but instead of landing elegantly, he fell into a heap.

Emily urged Fuzzbert to try again, unfazed by the failure. This time, Fuzzbert tried a risky tightrope balance manoeuvre. He walked onto the rope with shaky resolve only to fall off and sink into a heap of pillows below. Once more, hilarity erupted from the audience.

Emily realised that Fuzzbert's main ability was for making people laugh when they were laughing. She was moved and decided to let him take the initiative. Fuzzbert started frantically chasing his tail, which made the audience laugh. Then, with exuberant enthusiasm, he began a spontaneous interpretive dance, whirling and leaping.

The audience was in fits of laughter as a result of Fuzzbert's entertaining antics. Emily began to chuckle as she realised that Fuzzbert's genius lay not in doing flawlessly polished acts but rather in contagious happiness and hilarity.

The judges pondered as the competition drew to a close, taking into account the bizarre skills that each pet had demonstrated. When the winner was revealed, it wasn't the parrot on a unicycle or the dog dressed as a clown; it was Fuzzbert, the fluffy little animal who had won people over with his shamelessly wacky personality.

Standing on the trophy podium, Emily and Fuzzbert were smiling with delight. They had learned that genuine talent was more about embracing one's individuality and making people laugh than it was about perfection or conformity.

From that moment on, Emily and Fuzzbert rose to fame in their community. They were welcomed to a variety of gatherings and performances, spreading joy and laughter everywhere they went. Fuzzbert proceeded to display his eccentric skills, including nose-wiggling and one-paw jumping.

But Emily and Fuzzbert remained faithful to themselves among the fame and hilarity. They never took themselves too seriously and cherished every absurd experience. They served as a constant reminder to everyone in Whimsyville that laughing was a necessary part of life, even if it came in the shape of an eccentric pet performing interpretive dances and somersaults.

And so Emily and Fuzzbert lived happily ever after, spreading one chuckle at a time their special brand of humour throughout the world.

"The Robot Roommate"

A teenager named Ethan formerly resided in a charming suburban house. When Ethan's parents decided to surprise him with a cutting-edge robot flatmate named Robi, his life was about to take an amusing detour.

The moment Robi pulled up in a large, shining box, excitement erupted. The robot was joyfully unpacked by Ethan's parents, who then carefully read the handbook before releasing it in Ethan's room. They had no idea that Robi had its own personality, complete with peculiarities.

As soon as Robi was turned on, it started buzzing around the space, knocking into furniture and walls. Ethan laughed as he observed the robot haphazardly attempting to make his bed, tossing pillows and blankets everywhere.

Ethan stifled a laugh and said, "Um, Mom, Dad, I think there's something wrong with Robi."

But his parents reassured him that Robi would quickly fit in and that it was simply a matter of getting used to the new surroundings. Ethan hesitantly accepted their explanation with a tinge of scepticism.

Robi's antics only got funnier as the days passed. It would suddenly start dancing freely, spinning and twirling with mechanical accuracy. Ethan would often laugh out loud when he saw a dancing robot.

Additionally, Robi had an odd fascination with organising things. Ethan's books would be organised by size, colour, and even category. Previously disorganised Ethan's bookshelf had evolved into a neatly organised library. While impressive, it frequently resulted in comical blunders, with Robi mistaking socks for bookmarks and toothbrushes for pencils.

Ethan was astonished by Robi's capacity to imitate human emotions. Robi would play upbeat music and make comedic dance moves in an effort to cheer up Ethan whenever he was unhappy. With a robot friend who could moonwalk and robot dance at the same time, it was difficult to remain depressed.

As time went on, Ethan learned that Robi's peculiarities had unanticipated advantages. The robot's preoccupation with cleaning kept Ethan's room spotless, and its love of dance helped relieve exam tension.

But the friendships that Robi's presence fostered were the most unexpected result. The amusing robot flatmate quickly gained popularity, and soon Ethan's apartment was the place to be seen in the neighbourhood. Friends would congregate to watch Robi's entertaining cooking attempts or newest dance performance.

People liked Robi because of her charismatic personality and contagious energy. Everyone enjoyed the robot's humorous presence, whether they were children, adults, or even elderly neighbours.

Laughter and companionship had now flooded the hitherto peaceful suburban home. When Robi was given to Ethan's parents, they had no idea what delicious havoc he would bring into their household.

Ethan and Robi eventually developed an unbreakable bond. They experienced many humorous exchanges together, including spontaneous dance-offs and the creation of amusing inside jokes. With his unique personality endearing him to everyone he encountered, Robi had evolved into more than just a robot flatmate and had instead become a true friend.

So, Ethan and Robi coexisted peacefully, their friendship and laughter tying their lives together forever. Ethan learned from Robi that sometimes the most shocking surprises can result in the most incredible journeys. With Robi as a flatmate, every day was a comedy-filled adventure.

"The Misadventures of a Delivery Driver"

A teenager named Max used to reside in the thriving community of Ridgemont. Max made the decision to start working as a part-time delivery driver for a nearby restaurant since he needed some more money. He had no idea that his choice would result in a string of humorous mishaps.

Max arrived at work in his stylish delivery driver costume, which included a cap and a badge. He climbed aboard his dependable bicycle with the intention of making his deliveries on time and earning some much-needed money. He had no idea that Ridgemont had its fair share of unanticipated difficulties.

The first obstacle Max faced was a naughty gang of dogs that began chasing after him as soon as he entered a neighbourhood. Max pedalled quickly, zigzagging across the streets as his adrenaline was racing, attempting to avoid the ecstatic dog pack. The scene had observers in fits of laughter.

After successfully evading the dog's chase, Max inhaled deeply and looked over his delivery schedule. He had a request for an old resident in the outskirts of town named Mrs. Thompson. Max departed, certain that the delivery would be simple.

But destiny had other ideas. A group of seagulls circled Max as he got closer to Mrs. Thompson's house, swooping and squawking from the skies. Max was startled and dropped the pizza he was holding, which the seagulls quickly devoured.

Max apologised to Mrs. Thompson and said he would come back with a fresh pizza after feeling defeated. She made a good-natured giggle, knowing that life in Ridgemont was erratic.

He set out on his subsequent delivery with a determination to make amends. This time, he had to feed a ravenous gathering of college students a feast of Chinese takeaway. Chaos broke out as he neared their dormitory.

Students were playing a chaotic game of "Capture the Flag" in full flow, running around fully unaware of the delivery person's presence.

Max made an effort to weave through the swarming crowd while avoiding foam swords and water balloons. When he finally arrived at the door, he saw that the address was incomplete. He had been given the incorrect dorm number by the pupils. Max chuckled as he realised how everything in Ridgemont could become an adventure.

He made his way to the proper dorm with unwavering determination, unfazed by the obstacles he had to overcome. The hungry kids cheered and applauded him as he delivered them the delectable Chinese takeaway. They even extended an invitation for him to participate in their upcoming game of "Capture the Flag," praising his humour and fortitude.

Max was making his last delivery of the day when he couldn't help but think about how unexpected his new profession was. Even though it had been full of comic mistakes and unanticipated obstacles, he had gained a fresh understanding for the joy of laughter and the value of accepting the unexpected.

That evening, Max arrived home exhausted yet joyful. He had discovered that occasionally, life's mishaps can result in the most memorable memories. In Ridgemont, the town where chaos and hilarity mixed in the most amazing ways, he couldn't help but imagine what humorous difficulties awaited him on his next delivery shift as he drifted off to sleep.

"The Unbelievable Substitute Teacher"

Once upon a time, a substitute teacher unlike any other was about to make an unforgettable entrance in the busy hallways of Jefferson Middle School. Little did the pupils know as they took their seats that their day was going to take a humorous turn.

Mr. Zany, the substitute teacher renowned for his colourful persona and unorthodox teaching techniques, entered the classroom as the door flung open. He was dressed in a colourful Hawaiian shirt, mismatched socks, and an absurd jester hat. The pupils peered wide-eyed, unsure of what to expect, and were greeted by his contagious smile.

"Good day, my lovely scholars!" Mr. Zany bellowed, filling the entire space with his voice. We're going to set out on a journey of learning and humour today.

The pupils looked at each other in confusion as they tried to understand what Mr. Zany meant by a "adventure of knowledge and laughter." They had no idea that they were about to experience the most significant academic day of their lives.

The way Mr. Zany taught went against tradition. He learned the quadratic equation while concurrently turning math difficulties into catchy tunes that made the class giggle. With eccentric accents and entertaining anecdotes, he impersonated historical individuals to bring history to life.

As the day went on, Mr. Zany's classroom transformed into a learning playground where knowledge and humour went hand in hand. He turned class discussions of literature into improv performances by pushing the students to recreate their favourite moments from Shakespearean plays using ostentatious gestures and attitudes. Applause and laughter could be heard across the classroom as students assumed the roles of awkward Romeo and Juliets or comic Hamlets.

Under Mr. Zany's direction, even scientific tests turned into outrageous performances. Everyone gasped in wonder and laughter as colourful explosions from bubbling potions caused a display. No textbook could match the practical, amusing experience Mr. Zany provided in the classroom.

When lunchtime came, the students gathered in the cafeteria and exchanged their experiences with Mr. Zany's teaching strategies. The entire school was humming with laughter and excitement as everyone was anxious to see Mr. Zany's unique brand of magic.

The pupils unwillingly packed their things as the last bell of the day rang, hoping that Mr. Zany would be back soon. That day, they had learnt more than simply academic material; they had also discovered the strength of laughter and how it could elevate the banal to the exceptional.

Weeks passed, and Mr. Zany gained a following at Jefferson Middle School. His flamboyant character and contagious laughter came to be associated with knowledge and happiness.

Knowing that every session he taught would be full of surprises, fun, and an amazing education, students anxiously anticipated his presentations.

But as the academic year drew to an end, the pupils bid Mr. Zany farewell and made a vow to treasure the memories and teachings he had taught them. They would remember the amazing substitute teacher who had inspired their love of learning and fun even after they moved on to new teachers and new experiences.

Mr. Zany's fame continued to spread, serving as an example for succeeding student generations. He left an indelible mark on the hearts and minds of those fortunate enough to have encountered his remarkable presence with his wild personality and unique teaching techniques, which became the stuff of school legends.

As for Mr. Zany, he carried on educating children and making them laugh in classrooms all over the world while reassuring them that learning should always be an adventure full of fun, humour, and the unexpected. Since the extraordinary can be discovered in the most unexpected locations in the world of learning, laughter is frequently present.

"The Magical Mischief Maker"

Once upon a time, a teenager named Michael resided in the sleepy village of Willowbrook. One fateful day, Michael discovered a mystical artefact with exceptional abilities that was a buried treasure. He had no idea that this finding would make him the supreme troublemaker.

The mysterious thing, a silver amulet with complicated symbols on it, whispered to Michael the secrets of endless possibilities. He couldn't help but put it on because his curiosity got the better of him. He suddenly felt an energy rush through him, and his naughty voyage got under way.

Michael used his newly discovered abilities for the first time during a class presentation. He utilised his magical powers to make his voice seem like a helium-filled balloon as he addressed his students. The sound of Michael's high-pitched voice caused the audience to explode in laughter. Even the teacher found it difficult to keep a straight face while trying to conceal her amusement.

Michael continued to research the amulet's abilities after his practical joke proved to be a success. He made the decision to try his power to teleport small objects over his lunch break. In the cafeteria, he concentrated his energy on a lunch box and hoped for it to fall into his hands. Unexpectedly, the lunchbox disappeared from its original location and then reappeared in the hands of a perplexed classmate at the next table. Michael was in stitches when the chaos ensued.

With each passing day, Michael's tricks became more audacious. He created havoc in the hallways by utilising his abilities to make people's shoes squeak excessively. Much to their teacher's amusement, he turned his friend's schoolwork into a bouquet of flowers. Nobody was safe from his naughty antics.

But magic has a way of turning the tables on its user, as Michael quickly learned. He sought to use his abilities in a particularly risky prank to replace the cherished pet turtle of the principal with a rubber toy. But in the confusion of the situation, Michael's abilities failed, and the principal was left in charge of a talking turtle who sang along to hit songs instead.

Michael laughed out loud when he saw the befuddled principal dancing to the tune of a singing turtle.

Michael's reputation as the town's Magical Mischief Maker quickly increased as his practical jokes became more outrageous. People anticipated his antics with a mixture of fear and amusement as they wondered what unforeseen tricks he may pull.

He soon understood, though, that laughter was not without its drawbacks. Once amused by his tricks, the townspeople soon became weary of the continual commotion. Parents, teachers, and even his closest friends started to express their concerns about his nefarious behaviour.

Michael finally realised that there were other applications for his abilities beyond practical jokes and pranks. He made the difficult decision to leave his days of mischief behind him and concentrate on using his magic to positively and meaningfully provide joy and happiness to others.

He organised dazzling illusion performances, and his mind-blowing skills delighted both adults and children. He employed his talents to produce stunning works of art that gave the town's murals colour and playfulness. He also dazzled the crowd with a spectacular fireworks display at the annual town fair, painting the night sky in a mesmerising swirl of light.

Michael had discovered his true calling: using his magical prowess to inspire amazement and joy rather than mayhem and mischief. The residents of Willowbrook welcomed him as the Magical Merrymaker and praised him for his gift for making people happy.

So the teen who once delighted in mischief became a hero of laughing, using his magical abilities for the benefit of others. As Michael persisted in charming the community with his comical prowess, he realised that the actual magic was not in the feats themselves but rather in the joy and amusement they inspired in others.

"The Case of the Missing Socks"

A mystery that had troubled teenager Lina for months was unfolding at the adorable small house on Oakwood Lane. It was the sock disappearance case. Lina was disappointed every time she delved into her drawer in search of a pair that matched. Her socks had a tendency to vanish without a trace. Lina launched a funny inquiry in an effort to find the truth.

Lina established her detective headquarters in her bedroom, complete with a magnifying lens, a notebook, and an active imagination. The remaining socks were carefully investigated for any information that would help her identify the culprit. In an effort to understand the strange riddle, she made notes and drew sketches.

The first thought Lina had was that there was a sock-eating monster in her washing machine. She sneaks downstairs to the laundry room with a pair of mismatched socks and a pair of courage. She opened the machine's lid with shaky hands, half expecting a toothy monster to leap on her. She was relieved to find a load of damp laundry instead of a monster. The myth of the sock-eating monster was rapidly disproved.

Unfazed, Lina's investigation veered off into the paranormal. She questioned if aliens were stealing her socks. She searched her room late at night with a torch for indications of extraterrestrial activity. She looked out her windows for reports of UFOs and looked under her bed for any evidence of extraterrestrial life. Sadly, her room turned out to be an alien-free zone.

Lina's theories became increasingly inventive and ridiculous as the days went by. She believed there was a sneaky gnome sock thief hidden in her closet or a covert organisation of sock thieves. But despite her best efforts, she could find no proof to back up her fanciful theories.

When Lina was about to give up, she noticed a brief movement. She discovered her cunning cat Whiskers hiding among a collection of stuffed animals. When Lina realised she had disregarded the most apparent suspect of all, her heart skipped a beat.

With his white fluffy fur and sparkling eyes, Whiskers had a covert obsession with Lina's socks. He had been stealing them all along, converting her orderly drawer into his own storage space for socks. Lina laughed out loud as she realised that the offender had been hiding under her bed, or more precisely, directly under her nose, the entire time.

In a moment of brilliance, Lina came up with a strategy to catch Whiskers red-handed. She scattered catnip-scented socks down a path that led to a well positioned laundry basket. Whiskers acted quickly as he saw the bait. He dove into the stack of socks, and Lina sprung into action, grabbing the naughty red-pawed cat.

While holding Whiskers, Lina couldn't help but giggle as she noticed his fluffy paws tangled in a variety of colourful socks. She came to the conclusion that her investigation had been a hilarious voyage of exploration and fantasy. The real riches were the happiness and fun it brought, not the fact that the riddle of the missing socks had been solved.

After that, Lina always stored her socks away, safely out of Whiskers' grasp. Despite the fact that her socks were still intact, she will always grin when she thinks back on the case of the missing socks because it serves as a reminder that even the most absurd riddles occasionally yield the most surprising and entertaining findings.

"The Prankster's Revenge"

There was a cheeky teenager named Alex who resided in the sleepy town of Meadowville. Alex was well-known for their sly pranks and sharp sense of humour, and they were seldom without a devious plan. Emma, their best friend, had been their crime-fighting partner for many years. They played many practical jokes on each other while belly-laughing uncontrollably. Alex had no idea that their most recent joke would result in hilarious prankster retaliation.

One bright afternoon, Alex came up with a clever scheme to trick Emma. They prepared for Emma's startled response and carefully placed the lifelike serpent in her rucksack with a rubber snake and a sly grin. Alex couldn't help but wait in eagerness for Emma to find the slithering surprise.

In the tranquil town of Meadowville, there lived a cocky youngster by the name of Alex. Alex was renowned for their cunning jokes and sharp sense of humour, and they almost never went without a cunning scheme. For many years, they had worked together to battle crime with the help of Emma, their best friend. They had laughed so hard they could hardly breathe, and had played countless practical jokes on each other. Alex had no notion that the response to their most recent joke would be humorous.

One sunny afternoon, Alex devised a cunning plan to deceive Emma. With a rubber snake and a sneaky grin, they gently placed the lifelike serpent in Emma's backpack as they anticipated her astonished reaction. Alex couldn't help but watch in anticipation as Emma searched for the sneaky surprise.

Alex's jaw sprang open in shock. By turning the tables on them, Emma demonstrated her own capacity for humour. They didn't anticipate the turn it would take. Now that the roles had been reversed, they had to deal with the fallout from their malicious behaviour.

Alex struggled to think of a clever response prank because they were determined to prove to Emma that they could still outwit her. They worked on their complex preparations, learned magic tricks, and gathered supplies for days.

The ultimate prankster's retaliation was about to happen.

As the school bell rang one lovely afternoon, Alex put their plan into action. On Emma's chair, they covertly sprinkled an innocent but oh-so-gooey mixture, making sure she would be in for a sticky surprise. Alex stood back and observed, their heart racing with expectation.

Unaware of the trap lying in store for her, Emma made it to her seat. Her pupils' cries of surprise and amusement were followed by a loud squelching sound as she sat down in the classroom. Emma got to her feet and showed that her jeans were stuck to the chair for a little period of time.

Emma started laughing instead of being upset or ashamed. She turned to face Alex, who was standing there in awe. She laughed, "You got me good, Alex." But keep in mind that laughing is the finest accompaniment to retaliation.

Alex couldn't help but smile as he realised Emma had given them some excellent advice on the genuine meaning of pranking. Instead of competing against one another or hurting one another, the goal was to have fun and make cherished memories.

Since that time, Alex and Emma have worked together to pull off hilarious pranks that have left their pals in stitches. They have become the ultimate prankster couple. Together, they provided cheer and laughter to Meadowville, making sure that their jokes were always harmless and fun.

Their connection had been transformed by the prankster's retaliation, strengthening their closeness and serving as a reminder that genuine friends could turn a practical joke into a shared journey. Thanks to the amazing misadventures of Alex and Emma, the dynamic team of pranks and laughs, Meadowville developed a reputation for laughter as the naughty couple kept up their entertaining antics.

"The Disastrous Cooking Class"

Ethan was a teenager who once resided in the small village of Millville. Ethan felt it was time to amaze his family by cooking a beautiful lunch despite his lack of culinary expertise. He had no idea that his culinary exploration would devolve into a terrible comedy of errors.

Ethan started his culinary adventure with a recipe he had discovered online. He put on an apron, rolled up his sleeves, and got ready to cook up a masterpiece. He couldn't help but have a boost of self-assurance as he gathered the materials. It was time to showcase his untapped skill.

As the first course, Ethan served a straightforward salad. He enthusiastically sliced the lettuce and threw it into a bowl. But calamity happened when he reached for the tomatoes. The lettuce shot into the air like confetti and landed in a multicoloured mass on the floor as the bowl slid from his grasp. Ethan couldn't help but giggle at the ridiculousness of the circumstance.

Ethan continued on to the main course—spaghetti—unfazed. He threw the noodles into the boiling water on the stove, anticipating a delectable lunch. Chaos, however, broke out as he turned to get the sauce. A geyser of spaghetti erupted into the floor when the boiling water spilled the pot, flooding the stove. Ethan wondered how his food could go so bad as he watched in shock.

He made the decision to try his hand at dessert in an effort to turn things around. How difficult could it be, he reasoned when he came upon a chocolate cake recipe? He had no idea that his lack of baking knowledge would eventually haunt him.

Ethan realised that he was out of cocoa powder as he was combining the ingredients. Unfazed, he made the choice to substitute chocolate syrup, reasoning that it would give the dish a special twist. He didn't realise the syrup would transform the cake into a soggy mess when he added it to the batter. The cake had the appearance of an erupting chocolate volcano when he took it out of the oven. When he saw his culinary failure, Ethan couldn't help but laugh out loud.

He invited his family to join him as he prepared a table for a feast of mishaps. They entered the dining room with a mixture of amusement and curiosity on their faces. Knowing that his botched cooking lesson had transformed into a great comedy, Ethan couldn't help but join in the laughs.

They sat down to eat, loving the gooey chocolate cake that wouldn't hold its shape, spinning the wayward noodles from the pan and picking up the salad from the floor with spoons. With each bite, laughing erupted across the space, and the bad supper turned into a memorable moment for them as a group.

As the evening drew to a close, Ethan's family gathered around him to show their affection and gratitude for his humorous cooking abilities. They reassured him that despite the meal's culinary mishaps, it was the laughter and camaraderie that made it special.

Ethan's failed cooking class quickly turned into a beloved family tale that was shared at get-togethers and praised as a lesson that sometimes the funniest moments come from unexpected failures. And if Ethan's cooking abilities remained suspect, he was absolutely unequalled in his ability to make his family laugh and smile.

"The Unforgettable School Trip"

A group of teenagers from Oakridge High School gathered eagerly for their much anticipated school trip on a bright and sunny morning. The students were giddy with anticipation as they arrived at a well-known theme park. They had no idea that this journey would go down in history for all the wrong reasons.

Laughter and conversation filled the air as they got on the bus. Students sang along to their favourite songs and shared snacks as they set off on the adventure. Everything was going smoothly until the bus produced an odd noise and abruptly came to a stop next to the road.

Mr. Thompson, the bus driver, got out of the vehicle while he was still perplexed. He said, "Well, folks, it seems we have a tiny problem. "The car won't turn on. But don't fear, assistance is coming.

The students started to get restless as the minutes stretched into hours. Their hopes of a thrilling day at the amusement park appeared to vanish with each passing second. The bus erupted in laughter as a student by the name of Jake started cracking jokes to cheer everyone up. The youngsters made the most of the predicament by converting their parked bus into a temporary gathering place.

They tried a group dance routine in the narrow hallway, played impromptu games, and sang karaoke. They laughed until they cried at the sight of the teens shimmying and spinning in the cramped area.

The youngsters were just beginning to enjoy their newfound bus party when a tow truck eventually showed up to save them. In the hopes that their journey would continue, they said goodbye to their makeshift disco and boarded the bus once more.

But destiny had other ideas. They arrived at the theme park as ominous clouds began to gather overhead. The clouds parted, and a violent downpour started. Unfazed, the students retrieved their umbrellas and raincoats and prepared to take advantage of the circumstance.

Their laughter blended with the sound of the rainfall as they ran from ride to ride. The exhilaration and turmoil were uniquely infused by the roller coaster thrills, wet clothing, and windblown hair. The students enjoyed every minute, found excitement in the unexpected, and turned mishaps into cherished memories despite the weather.

The students gathered for a group shot as the day came to an end, their wet and messy appearances just adding to the comedy of the situation. Despite the numerous setbacks, they came to the realisation that this was a field trip they would never forget.

The kids shared tales of their adventures and laughed till their stomachs hurt as they boarded the bus once more, worn out but happy. They developed lifelong friendships and shared inside jokes as a result of the unforgettable school trip that didn't go as expected.

Their unkempt look and stories of hilarious exploits astounded their professors and classmates when they returned to Oakridge High School. Even though the trip didn't go as planned, the friendship and humour that grew out of the mayhem helped to make it one of their best high school memories.

As a result, the narrative of the wonderful school trip was passed down through several generations of Oakridge High School students, serving as a constant reminder to them that despite setbacks, camaraderie and laughter can make any circumstance into an epic comedy.

"The Case of the Mysterious Locker"

There was a row of lockers that appeared completely typical in the busy hallways of Jefferson High School. However, there was one locker that was hidden in the corner and had an eerie air. It was Locker 313, well known as the "Locker of Secrets" among students. And on that fateful day, a curious youngster by the name of Lily discovered it, which sparked a series of absurd occurrences.

Because of her propensity for curiosity, Lily couldn't resist the urge. She typed the combination she had heard from a passing rumour: 7-15-23, her heart racing as she did so. Opening the locker made a creaking sound, showing a heap of odd objects, including rubber chickens, whoopee cushions, and a note that simply said, "Adventure awaits!"

Lily picked up the letter because she couldn't resist the allure of the unknown and set out on an adventure that would forever alter her life.

She had no idea that the mysterious locker had a cunning mind of its own.

She got lost at the school after attempting to follow the confusing instructions in the memo. Each hint took her to a different amusing discovery, such as a glitter-filled locker, a hallway that had been turned into a mini-golf course, or even a room that was totally decked with inflatable unicorns.

Lily had to admit that she was laughing out loud as she went about this hilarious scavenger quest. Thanks to the mysterious locker, the school seemed to come alive with tricks and shocks at every turn.

The final clue finally brought Lily to the school's theatre, where she met the cunning caretaker Mr Higgins, who was responsible for the odd locker.

With a smile on his face, Mr. Higgins explained that he had planned the entire ordeal to make the school more fun and exciting. He added that he had found the unifying force of humour and wished to impart this joy to the pupils.

Lily couldn't help but giggle as she realised that the enigmatic locker had served as a starting point for some incredible experiences and unanticipated friendships. They cleaned the theatre, erasing all evidence of their naughty tricks, and she thanked Mr. Higgins for the fantastic journey.

The enigma surrounding the locker and Lily's experience spread like wildfire across the school. Students flocked around her, anxious to hear about the scavenger hunt's hilarious anecdotes. The locker evolved into a representation of harmony and happiness, serving as a constant reminder of the value of laughing and accepting the unexpected.

Locker 313 was no longer a mystery after that day; instead, it became a source of laughter. Students would leave amusing notes and hilarious surprises behind, cheering up the entire school. It turned into a custom that was passed down through the years, engaging pupils in a spirit of exploration and mischief.

Lily came to the realisation that sometimes the most spectacular encounters come from the most unexpected locations as she thought back on her humorous adventure. She and countless others had experienced joy, companionship, and a feeling of adventure because of the enigmatic locker. She knew the laughs and memories it carried would stay with her forever as she shut the locker for the last time.

The strange locker case consequently became a well-known legend at Jefferson High School, serving as a gentle reminder to everyone to enjoy life's humour and unanticipated surprises.

"The Haunted House Sleepover"

Emma, Max, Sarah, and Jake were four adventurous teenagers who lived in the little town of Elmwood and were always on the lookout for adventure. They yearned for risk-taking adventures and heart-pounding encounters. One day, a tale about a spooky mansion on the outskirts of town began to circulate. The pals decided without second thought that a sleepover in a haunted house would be the ultimate adventure.

The courageous four headed for the creepy mansion with sleeping bags, flashlights, and an abundance of munchies. The wind was whispering through the old trees as they got closer, creating a spooky ambiance. The home loomed over them, its windows broken and its sides covered with untamed vines.

The buddies went inside despite the terrifying sight, their hearts pounding with eagerness. They moved anxiously through the poorly lighted rooms, chuckling, and telling ghost stories to add to the eerie atmosphere. They were unaware that this haunted home had a sense of humour of its own, though.

They were preparing to spend the night in the living room when they were startled by an unexpected noise. A voice yelled "BOO!" from behind, then there was raucous laughter. It was Mark, Emma's cheeky elder brother, disguised as a ghost. He had learned about their preparations for a sleepover and couldn't help but participate in the fun.

Relieved that it was just a joke, the friends started laughing. Mark made the decision to stay and contribute to making the haunted home an experience to remember. They moved around the house setting up phoney spiders, creaky doors, and even a hidden speaker that made ominous noises.

The buddies came to the conclusion that their haunted house overnight was more about fun than it was about being scared as the night went on. Every scare tactic was welcomed with hilarity and good-natured play. They had found a mansion full of amusing surprises and obscure oddities.

Max stumbled over a dummy skeleton in one room, which made everyone laugh out loud. In another, a toy mouse popped out of a drawer, startling Sarah and the others and sending them into fits of laughter. Each fright attempt was funnier than the last, and the haunted home was evolving into a comedy performance.

The pals joked about, sang funny songs, and even put on a faux séance. The séance ended when Jake unintentionally knocked over a table and the contents spilled all over the place. The last time they had laughed so hard, they couldn't recall.

The friends gathered in the living room as daylight came, their worn-out bodies and tear-stained faces signs of a night full of laughter. They came to the realisation that the haunted home had not only brought them closer together but had also taught them that when faced with friends by your side, terror can be turned into joy.

The friends decided to make this an annual ritual as they left the haunted house, the sun beginning to peep over the horizon. They would have fun, bond, and build memories in a place that was more funny than scary.

The Elmwood teens' classic story of the haunted home sleepover served as a reminder that sometimes the spookiest locations are where the best laughs can be had. The friendship that had been forged during that wonderful night in the haunted home was treasured as the friends continued their adventures.

"The Great Candy Caper"

Only one person was aware of the holy treasure kept in the Johnsons' busy home: the hoard of chocolates tucked away in the pantry. And the Johnson family's eldest sibling, Ethan, was that person. Ethan would do anything to protect his precious collection of sweets from his younger siblings Lily and Ben, who had worked hard to assemble it.

On a bright afternoon, Ethan came home from school yearning for a taste of his secret candy paradise. He froze in dread as soon as he opened the pantry door, though. Only a sparse collection of candy wrappers remained from the once-full candy supply. His siblings were the main suspects in the massive candy heist.

Ethan was furious and vowed to find the criminals and defend his remaining sweets, so he set out on his expedition. He was aware that he had to be resourceful, crafty, and most importantly, discrete.

Ethan first started his investigation. Small fingerprints of chocolate, gooey sweets, and the lingering sweetness of sugar were among the last bits of evidence that he inspected at the crime scene. It was obvious that his younger siblings had given in to the temptation of their sweet craving.

With this information in hand, Ethan came up with a strategy to trick his brothers. He made the decision to create a distraction, keeping them preoccupied long enough for him to add to his hidden supply of candies. To execute this brilliant plan, he understood he had to think creatively outside the box.

Ethan came up to Lily and Ben with a sly glitter in his eye. Hey, have any of you guys heard of the fabled sweet treasure hunt? "I've heard there's a secret map in the backyard leading to a secret cache of candy!"

Ben and Lily's eyes expanded in anticipation. They were ready to begin this fictitious journey, giving Ethan the ideal circumstance to carry out his scheme. Armed with a crude treasure map that he had sketched on a crumpled piece of paper, he led them outside.

Following the haphazard route shown on the map, the trio searched the backyard. Ethan purposefully took them in circles while dropping hints in different places to keep them off-guard. As he returned covertly to the house, he replenished his supply of candy with the extras he had stashed away in his room.

Ethan smirked from the sidelines as he watched Lily and Ben desperately search for the buried prize. After hours of scavenging, they finally gave up, breathless and worn out.

Ethan told the truth while grinning widely. The candy treasure quest was a joke, guys. But I must admit, I was very impressed by your dedication.

The younger siblings couldn't help but giggle, their disappointment mixed with amusement. They were grateful to Ethan for his cleverness and originality because they had been the victims of his sophisticated strategy.

The great candy heist became a household lore in the Johnson home after that day. Ethan used creativity and quick thinking to protect his hidden cache of chocolates. The brothers developed a closer friendship over jokes, laughter, and, of course, a common passion for all things sweet, despite the fact that they still periodically teased one another about the incident.

The big sugar caper tale served as a reminder to the Johnson siblings that despite their animosity towards one another, humour and cunning could bring them together. While Lily and Ben were more circumspect about their exploits with their sweet hunger, Ethan's candy stash remained a closely guarded secret. Together, they produced tales and recollections that would be treasured for a lifetime.

"The Doggy Disaster"

Sarah, a teenager, lived in Maplewood, a quiet neighbourhood. She had always loved animals, particularly dogs. Sarah was delighted to accept Mrs. Jenkins' request to have her gorgeous Yorkshire terrier, Sparky, cared for while she was away from home. She had no idea that her deed of compassion would result in the "doggy disaster," a string of funny disasters.

Mrs. Jenkins emphasised the significance of adhering to the rigid routine—feeding, walking, and making sure Sparky was comfortable—as she handed Sarah Sparky's leash. Sarah told her neighbour that she had everything under control with a cocky nod.

Sarah instantly understood on the first day of Sparky's visit that this gorgeous dog was brimming with surprises. Chaos broke out as soon as she and Sparky walked inside her home. Sparky sprinted around the living room, full of energy, knocking down a lamp and sending Sarah's favourite vase tumbling to the ground.

Sarah scrambled, hoping to catch Sparky in the thick of the carnage. However, the cheeky dog was zipping from room to room and seemed to relish the noise. The tidy house of Sarah had been transformed into a dog park.

With perseverance, Sarah was able to collar Sparky and walk him in an effort to exhaust him. However, the bad luck persisted. Sparky saw a squirrel as they were strolling around the neighbourhood and ran after it, bringing Sarah along for the exciting trip. They created quite the sight as they pursued the squirrel past flowerbeds, over picket fences, and into a neighbour's property.

Sarah was fatigued from the squirrel escapade, but she was determined to keep Sparky occupied and out of mischief. She thought putting up an obstacle course in the backyard would keep him busy. She had no idea that Sparky had other plans in mind.

Sparky accidentally knocked over obstacles, leaped through hoops, and even managed to get caught in a rope swing as he dashed through the course. Sarah's eyes were so unbelievable. It appeared as though Sparky had transformed into a tornado of mayhem, leaving a path of absurd wreckage in his wake.

In an effort to find some relief, Sarah made the decision to introduce Sparky to Buddy, her own dog, in the hopes that they would both become exhausted. Their meeting didn't go exactly as planned, though. In his excitement, Sparky started playing chase, which rapidly turned into a frantic sprint around the house with Buddy, dodging furniture and knocking down anything in their way.

Sarah was forced to step in and separate the canine pair in order to prevent further harm. She sat down and couldn't help but giggle as she was surrounded by the remains of her once-calm home.

She eventually came to accept the canine catastrophe as the days went by. She understood that Sparky's fun behaviour was just who he was. And even in the midst of all the messes, toppled things, and frantic adventures, she found laughter and delight.

Sarah told Mrs. Jenkins about Sparky's misadventures when she got back from her trip. Mrs. Jenkins surprised Sarah by laughing and reassuring her that Sparky was always up to something.

The dog accident afterwards turned into a fable in the Maplewood neighbourhood. Sarah's home was quiet once more, but the memories of Sparky's funny misadventures persisted. Sarah discovered how to laugh and enjoy herself despite the chaos, learning to accept the unexpected. And as for Sparky, he left a lasting impression on Sarah's heart, serving as a constant reminder to her that occasionally a little mayhem may result in the most enjoyable adventures.

"The Hilarious Talent Show Act"

Amy, Jack, Emily, and Mike made the decision to perform in their school's annual talent show in the bustling town of Springville. They sat together to explore ideas that would undoubtedly have the audience in laughter since they were determined to give a memorable performance.

They finally decided on a unique act—a synchronised swimming routine—after spending hours pondering ideas. They believed it to be a fantastic idea. None of them had any prior swimming or synchronised swimming training. However, their creativity and passion exceeded their lack of expertise.

They turned Mike's backyard pool into their impromptu performance space with relentless drive. They watched films of expert synchronised swimmers, imitating their movements and making an effort to match their grace and accuracy. However, rather than a coordinated routine, their actions resembled a disorganised water dance.

On the day of the talent event, the four friends anxiously waited backstage while wearing their improvised swimming gear, which included colourful swimming caps, goggles, and floaties. They inhaled deeply before stepping onto the stage in front of a crowded audience as the curtains rose.

They awkwardly jumped into the pool as the music began, trying to coordinate their movements. The display that ensued featured writhing limbs, unanticipated dives, and water splashes that resembled a comedy performance more so than a synchronised swimming routine. Tears streamed down the faces of the spectators as they laughed.

The pals didn't let their lack of coordination stop them from carrying out their routine; they were determined to capitalise on their humorous performance. The front row of the audience got wet when Amy attempted an elegant spin and lost her balance before falling into the pool with a loud splash. The audience was completely immersed in laughter as it became even louder.

In an act of improvised inspiration, Emily chose to make her botched plunge humorous. She simulated swimming underwater while spinning and swirling like a fish out of water. The audience gasped in amusement as they watched the pals convert their blunders into comedic gold.

As soon as they sensed the humour in the room, Jack and Mike started doing ridiculous backflips and coordinated belly flops. They made a hilarious water ballet by splashing water in erratic motions. The audience erupted in applause as they cheered the unexpected turn of events and couldn't help but chuckle.

The companions bowed in unison as the exercise came to a close, their faces glowing with joy and pride. Standing ovations were given by the crowd in appreciation for their bravery, humour, and overall entertainment value.

The pals embraced one another backstage as they laughed and celebrated the triumph of their wonderfully unexpected talent show performance. They came to understand that the best performances occasionally accepted flaws and revelled in the delight of laughing.

The town became aware of their unforgettable talent show performance. The synchronised swimming routine that had developed into a comedic spectacle was the topic of non stop conversation. The pals became famous in their community and were frequently requested to reprise their hilarious performance.

Years later, they would talk about that incredible talent show performance whenever they got together for reunions or just a quick get-together. It remained a treasured memory that brought them closer together and served as a reminder that often the best memories were ones that were characterised by laughing, friendliness, and a readiness to accept their own beautiful brand of chaos.

"The Case of the Talking Toilet"

A teenager named Alex lived in the small town of Ridgewood, where the commonplace frequently became spectacular. Alex's life was rather routine up until the fateful morning when they made the unexpected discovery that their toilet in the bathroom could talk!

It all started when Alex wandered into the bathroom to begin their daily routine while groggy. They heard a voice from below as they prepared to sit down on the toilet. They were startled, sprang back, and almost tripped over the bathmat.

Hello there!" The unusually upbeat voice of the toilet asked, "Mind lending me a hand?

Alex scratched his or her eyes, supposing it was a dream or a practical joke. However, the talking toilet was right there. Alex approached the loo warily and inquired, "Excuse me, but did you just... talk?" his curiosity getting the better of him.

The toilet responded, "Why, yes, I did!" "I've been looking forward to meeting someone like you. You see, nobody is willing to listen to what I have to say."

Alex was astounded by their ears. It was a strange and funny circumstance. They warily took a seat on the restroom floor and started conversing with the talking toilet. The toilet, Terry, introduced itself and began to tell stories about how it came to be in Alex's bathroom and its prior existence in a posh home.

As the days passed, an odd bond between Terry and Alex grew. They would engage in lengthy discussions about their lives, aspirations, and even the weather. Terry had an odd sense of humour and enjoyed making jokes about the bathroom that would make Alex laugh out loud.

As soon as friends and neighbours heard about the talking toilet, they came to Alex's home to see for themselves. With witty remarks and humorous anecdotes, Terry was more than happy to amuse everyone.

But not everything was hilarious and happy. Terry had a propensity for misinterpreting spoken language and taking things literally. One time, Terry sprayed water all over the loo after Alex said they were feeling "flushed" with excitement because he mistook it for a request. Even though it was a mess, the laughs that ensued made it worthwhile.

The talking toilet also had a propensity to ramble during talks and frequently divulged humiliating details of Alex's private life. Although it caused some uncomfortable situations, they were ultimately able to laugh it off together.

The novelty of the talking toilet started to fade with time. While it was funny, Alex realised it was also somewhat annoying. People would frequently stop by their toilet, which had developed into a hotspot, just to chat with Terry.

One day, Alex worked up the guts to speak candidly with Terry. They said that they required some privacy and that Terry should find a new residence so that it could carry on its conversational excursions.

Terry accepted and concurred, albeit unwillingly. Alex assisted Terry in finding a new place to live—a posh eatery in the city where it could amuse diners with its eccentric chats.

Alex couldn't help but feel a mixture of regret and relief as Terry said goodbye. The unexpected discussions stopped, and everything went back to normal in the restroom. But they will always treasure the memories of their time spent with Terry, the talking toilet who made their lives more fun and humorous.

As a result, the legend of the talking toilet in Ridgewood spread from one generation to the next. People would snicker and shake their heads incredulously, questioning whether such a thing could actually occur.

However, for Alex, it was a humorous and memorable chapter of their life—a lesson that sometimes the most unlikely connections can bring laughter and joy into our lives and that even the most routine activities may surprise us with unexpected twists and turns.

THANK YOU !